MY MANNEQUINS

by
Sydell Waxman

illustrated by
Patty Gallinger

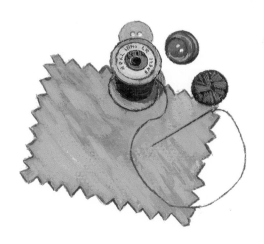

NAPOLEON PUBLISHING

Napoleon Publishing/RendezVous Press
Toronto, Ontario, Canada

Le Conseil des Arts | The Canada Council
du Canada | for the Arts

Napoleon Publishing gratefully acknowledges the support of the
Canada Council for the Arts for our publishing program.

Printed in Canada

10 09 08 07 06 05 04 03 02 01 00   5 4 3 2 1

Canadian Cataloguing in Publication Data

Waxman, Sydell, date-
    My mannequins

ISBN 0-929141-73-3

I. Gallinger, Patty. II. Title.

PS8595.A8779M9 2000   jC813'.6   C00-931970-0
PZ7.W3513My2000

To Allan, with much love, for being there
through all the stories, both fact and fiction.
– SW

For my husband Mark, whose unfailing input and patience
have steered my craft into the 21st century.
And for my father, who loved my paintings long before I did.
– PG

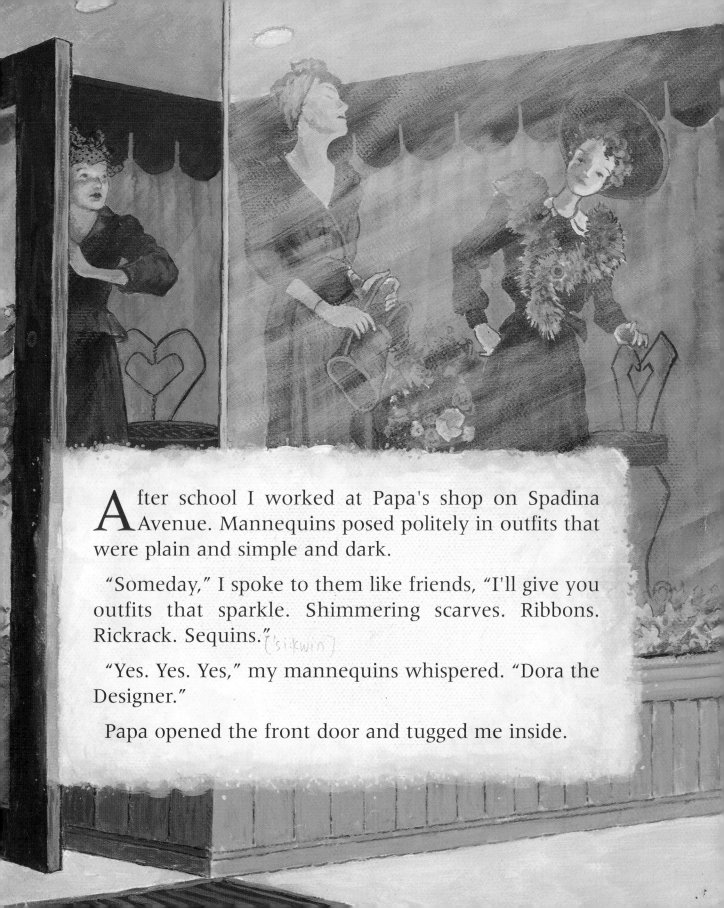

After school I worked at Papa's shop on Spadina Avenue. Mannequins posed politely in outfits that were plain and simple and dark.

"Someday," I spoke to them like friends, "I'll give you outfits that sparkle. Shimmering scarves. Ribbons. Rickrack. Sequins." ['siːkwin]

"Yes. Yes. Yes," my mannequins whispered. "Dora the Designer."

Papa opened the front door and tugged me inside.

"Dora, my daydreamer, we need you to make boxes. NOW."

Down I plunked onto the oak floor. Cross-legged, I sat caged by box tops and bottoms. My fingers flew, folding sides, pressing hard, slipping tabs all the way through the holes. I was a very good box-maker.

Then Jack, the cutter, taught me how to make
notches so that Edna and Isabella could match up
the pattern pieces.

Just as I was about to show Papa my notches, he turned, his voice booming across the bolts: "Production! Production!"

His voice was like a key turning the shop's engine.

Miss Avery drew faster, designing her pretty, plain pictures.

Jack opened his scissors wide. Then he scribbled on each puzzle piece. Dress 1 Front. Dress 1 Back.

What if I switched them? Wouldn't a backwards dress be fun?

"Papa." I peeked around the bolts. "What about a backwards dress?"

"Dora," he said, flatly, as if that were an answer, but my mannequins listened.

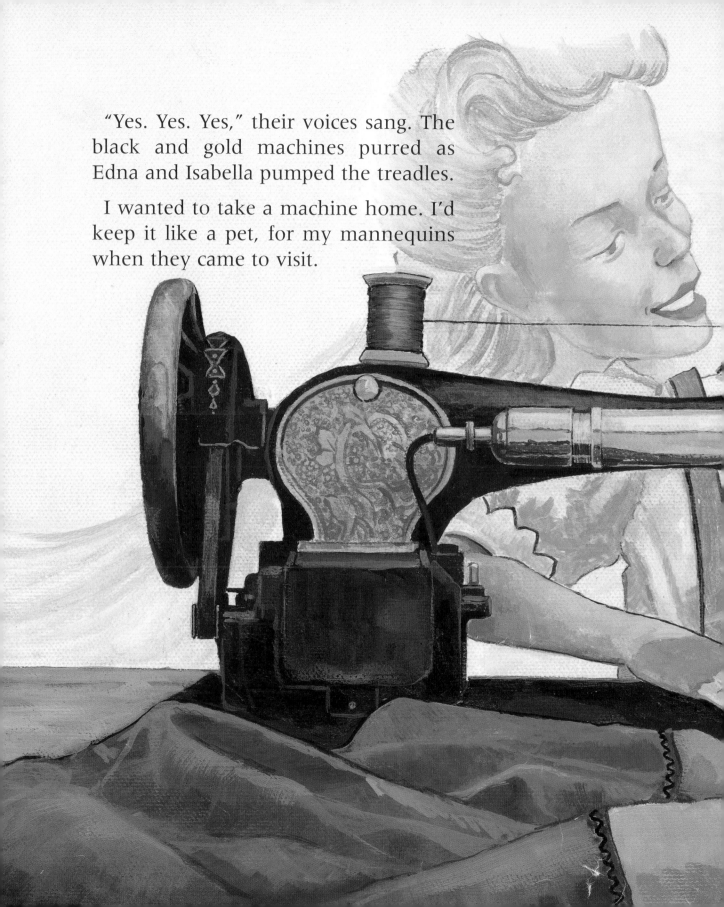

"Yes. Yes. Yes," their voices sang. The black and gold machines purred as Edna and Isabella pumped the treadles.

I wanted to take a machine home. I'd keep it like a pet, for my mannequins when they came to visit.

At breaktime, I practised pushing the material through the bouncing needles. My toes tingled with the swaying treadles.

"This will be for you," I said to one mannequin, adding pink to the red scarf.

Again, Papa's voice cut the air. "Production! Dora, we need more boxes. NOW."

When the boxes were done, I decorated the scarf with brocade ribbon.

"That's cute," said Edna as she prepared to leave for the day.

"Interesting," said Isabella, whipping by.

"Oh, never," said Miss Avery. "You never put pink and red together."

"Why not?" I asked. Miss Avery shrugged as she pinned her hat in place. She waved good-bye, but Papa didn't wave back. He had already switched to his evening job, reading reams of paper.

Soon, dusk darkened our two windows. Without sunlight, my mannequins looked really sad.

"You need some colour, some zest, some style."

"Yes. Yes. Yes," my mannequins chimed as I dug deep to the bottom of the remnant pile. Squeezing Jack's big scissors, I shaped and sheered. Fabric dust tickled my nose.

Papa didn't notice how lovely my mannequins looked. His head was stuck between paper piles. "What about me?" another mannequin asked.

Only black and brown and tattered blue pieces remained. I searched in the trash pails, under the bolts and between the machines. The notions shelf behind Papa glittered with sequins, tassels and rickrack trim.

Just as I tapped Papa on the shoulder to ask permission, his face tightened with thought.

"Yes. Yes. Yes." My mannequins winked. I sewed the sequins onto a black scrap and stretched the fabric over a bent hanger. "A hat with pizazz." Moonlight bounced off every sequin.

"Now you look fine. Much better indeed."

Threaded wood spools and buttons made chunky necklaces.

"You look fit for tea time," I said, placing cups in their hands. "Papa, would you like some tea?" I called. No answer.

My mannequins sipped and chatted.

"You look spiffy, my dear."

"Stylish!" I giggled.

Just then, Murphy, the cleaner, shuffled into our shop. Murphy's arrival was my signal. I, too, had to clean up.

My hands wound like a threader, twirling the rickrack back into a ball.

But much earlier than usual, Papa's squeaky chair slid away from his desk. "That's it," Papa said, tapping his hat in place. "Come along, Dora."

My throat tightened as if I'd swallowed a spool.

"Papa, I have to clean up the window display."

"That's Murphy's job," Papa said as he marched out the back door.

My head sizzled. How could I leave my mannequins this way? Would Papa be furious in the morning? Would he ban me from the shop?

"Come along, Dora," I heard Papa shout from the back lane. Slowly, sadly, I trudged home.

The next day, I couldn't wait for school to end.

Zooming along Spadina Avenue, I dodged speeding clothes racks. Hung thick with garments, the racks ran as if they had feet. I ran too. Had Edna and Isabella laughed and set things right? Maybe Papa had already forgotten the morning shock.

Finally, I neared our shop. My chest flapped like thin fabric when I saw all the people.

Murmurs spread through the crowd. "This is ridiculous."

"Outrageous."

But one voice was soft like silk. "Wait, take a look at this scarf."

"Mmm." said a buyer. "Creative."

"Daring." said one lady.

"Innovative." said another.

Had this been going on all day? Then, our front door flew open. Papa looked bigger and taller.

"Dora, we've been waiting for you. We left the mannequins in your, your..."

"Creations." I said.

"Well, whatever you call them." Papa's face was stern and steady.

I waited, my eyes downcast.

"We left them because people seem to like...the scarf. I don't know *why*, but they like the scarf."

My mouth dropped open. My mannequins cheered.

"Dora the Designer. Yes. Yes. Yes."

Papa rubbed his chin.

He stared as if seeing me clearly for the first time. Then waving his finger, he said: "You... you... you are..."

I nodded. "Dora the Designer!" I said.

Then a strange thing happened. A smile like a taut thread crinkled Papa's cheeks.

"Yes," Papa agreed, mouthing the words ever so slowly, "you are Dora...the Designer."

My happy heart roared like a racing machine. The sound bounced off the walls and mixed with the chugging Singers. Growing louder and louder, the music drowned the voices of my mannequins.

I spun around, wanting to hug them, but my mannequins looked cold and stiff. They had frozen, smiling at Papa's finger which was still going up and down.

"Well, let the customers in," Papa said.

Huge bolts of red and pink fabric flowed across the tables. Edna and Isabella sewed patch on patch until long scarves draped onto the floor.

"Production! Production!" I called with Papa.

Now, whenever Papa works late, when the Singers go silent and dusk darkens our two windows, I still hear the words. I smile at my stiff mannequins, and they smile back, but I know they can't answer.

It's my own voice I hear, saying, "Dora the Designer. Yes. Yes. Yes."

HISTORICAL NOTE

My Mannequins could easily have been a true story. During the first half of the twentieth century, thousands of children like Dora grew up in the bustling garment districts of Canada.

The garment trade was run mainly by Jewish immigrants who had fled persecution in countries such as Poland and Russia. Hopeful that their lives in Canada would be free of intolerance, they found, instead, that many job ads stated: "Gentiles only need apply."

The clothing business was one of the few industries that welcomed these newcomers. Labouring in factories such as the T. Eaton plant, workers were paid by "piecework" rather than by the hour. The more garments they made, the more money they earned. Some, like Dora's father in the story, finally saved enough for a press iron, material, and a Singer—the ultimate sewing machine.

Small dress shops sprouted around Spadina Avenue in Toronto. Similar garment areas developed in Winnipeg and Montreal. These shops established a vibrant Canadian industry and for decades supplied clothing and textiles to the entire country.

The industry dissipated in the 1950s as the children of these immigrants chose business and professional careers beyond the fashion districts. Canada's doors of tolerance had opened, leading to educational and business opportunities for all.

Like the Mannequins' voices, echoes of this era can still be heard. For people like Dora, the sewing machines roar on forever, having found a permanent place in their hearts and memories.

Sydell Waxman's eclectic career has encompassed work as a teacher, historical researcher, school librarian, lecturer and writer. She teaches creative writing in the Toronto area where she also gives many lively and informative school presentations. As a young girl, Sydell made boxes in her father's dress shop.

Her other publications include *Changing the Pattern: The Story of Emily Stowe* (Napoleon Publishing 1997) and *The Rooster Prince* (Pitsopany Press 2000).

Patty Gallinger has lived and pursued her art education in the Toronto area for most of her life, where she now lives with her husband and two small children. She began her professional career as a book designer, but for the last couple of years, she has concentrated on book illustration, particularly for children.

In her leisure time, she enjoys photography, gardening and writing.